This book belongs to

....

....

....

First Published 2017 by Ballynafagh Press
Ballynafagh, Prosperous, Naas, Co. Kildare, Ireland

ISBN: 978-0-9935792-1-9

Text © 2017 Emma-Jane Leeson
www.emmajaneleeson.com
Illustrations © 2017 Kim Shaw

Edited by Aoife Barrett
Design and Layout by Kim Shaw

Johnny Magory
and the Game of Rounders

Emma-Jane Leeson

For Lorna, Sarah and Pádraig...
But especially Sarah -
my secret weapon!

I'll tell you a story about Johnny Magory,
And the adventures he has with his trusty dog Ruairi.

He's a clever boy who's six years old,

He's **usually** good,

but he's

sometimes

bold!

Every year around July, it's time for Johnny to go to the bog,
To get the turf and bring it home to warm his family

...and the dog!

In wintertime in Ireland, it can be very, icy cold,
So, you cut your turf from the peat, a tradition from old.

J ohnny gets his exploring clothes, his **wellies** and his orange hat,

He helps his Mammy pack **sandwiches** and some **drinks** to go with that.

With sun cream on and insect spray, they all hop into the Jeep,

And with trusty Ruairi strapped in too, they head off with a ...

Beep-Beep!

Once they arrive, Mammy and Daddy waste no time,

Getting to work, footing the turf up and down the line!

And as Johnny is helping,

he hears a familiar sound,

He knows **exactly** who it is

before he even turns around.

It's **Finn the hare**, his good old friend, **boxing** the air,

He gestures to Johnny and Ruairi to follow him **if they dare!**

Finn Hare is super-quick as they chase him through the purple heather,
They run so fast the bog cotton rises as if it's stormy weather.
They jump the ditches and climb the piles as quickly as they can,
"Where's Finn Hare taking us?" Johnny wonders, "what's his plan?"

They hear cheering in the distance, it sounds like **tons** of fun,

Johnny and Ruairi **can't wait** to find out what's at the end of this run.

They race around a gorse bush and stop dead in their tracks;

All their animal friends are there, holding red baseball bats!

They're having a game of **rounders** with batters, bases and the rest,

Lord Stag is the

pitcher, Ms Squirrel on his back -

teamwork at its best!

Johnny **loves** rounders, he can't believe his **good luck**,

He asks the guys,

Lord Stag and Ms Squirrel **fire** the sliothar,

Johnny **belts** it with his bat,

And off he runs **as fast as he can**, around the first and second mat.

He's heading towards the **third base** and Johnny's pretty sure he's safe,
But Mr Frog **catches** the ball and he has his leg in the right place!

You're out!

he shouts to Johnny,
"hard luck, mo chara,"
he chatters.

Not to worry,

grins Johnny,
"it's playing, not winning,
that matters!"

Mr Frog is next up to take the bat and he really **belts** the ball,

Ms Grouse and Hen Harrier **scramble** to catch it, hoping not to fall.

Their eyes are busy in the air and not on the ground,

They **tumble** into each other and feathers **flutter** around!

And when Lord Stag gets up to bat, he does it with a mighty swoop,
He's so eager to get to first base that he trips over his hoof!

Bump!

Finn Hare is quick as a flash
and gets the fastest ever home run,
By zipping by all the bases,
to huge cheers from everyone!

The hours are **flying** by because Johnny is having such fun,

The dragonflies are **dancing** to celebrate each home run.

But Ruairi has **super hearing**
and he can hear a faint shout,
It doesn't take him long to realise
it's Mammy and Daddy giving out!

"Woof! Woof!"

It's time to go. Mammy was **yelling** for them.

"Oh no,"
says Johnny,

I'm going to be in trouble again!

Finn Hare brings them back to where they first set out,
Johnny sees his Ma and Da searching **frantically** about.

He gets into a bit of trouble for not doing his work;
It's all hands on deck when you're **footing the turf!**

He says he's "really sorry" but he winks at Ruairi with a grin,

How could he have passed up a game of rounders with Finn?!

Mammy lays out the picnic blanket and Daddy pours the tea flask,

They sit down to have their lunch in the beautiful purple moor grass.

The End

Let's continue the adventure with
the audio version book that's
waiting for you at
www.johnnymagory.com/listen

www.emmajaneleeson.com